Shel Silverstein

The Missing Piece Meets the Big O

HarperCollins*Publishers*

to Joan

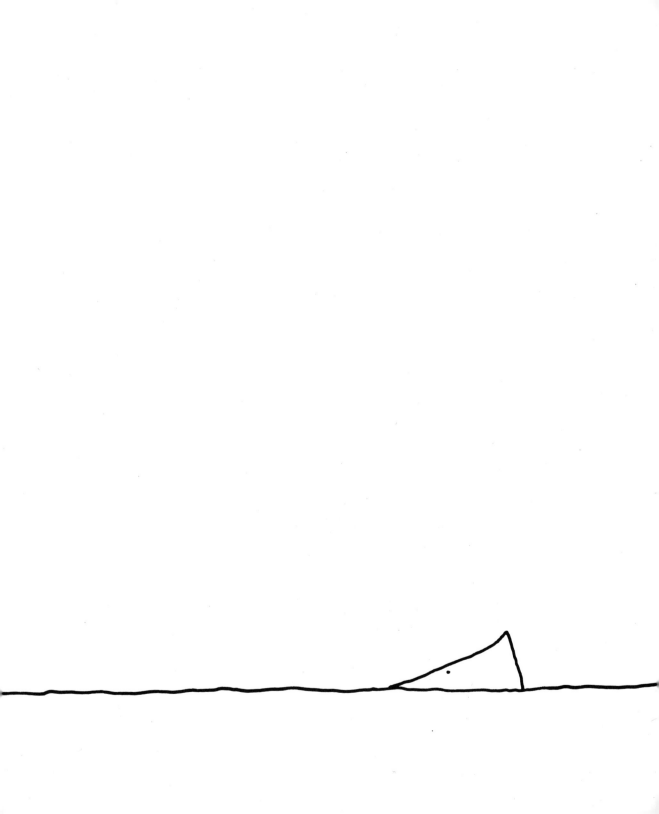

The missing piece sat alone...

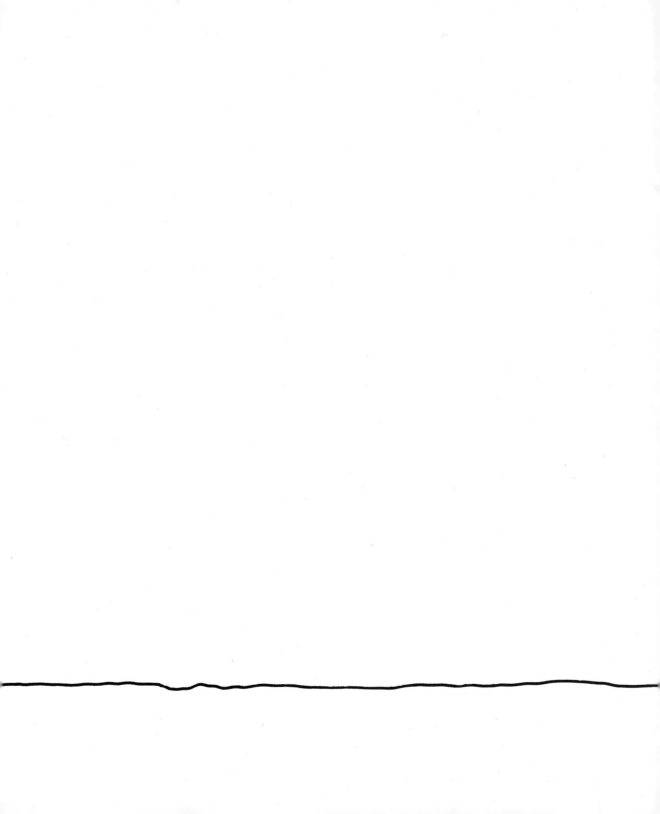

waiting for someone
to come along
and take it somewhere.

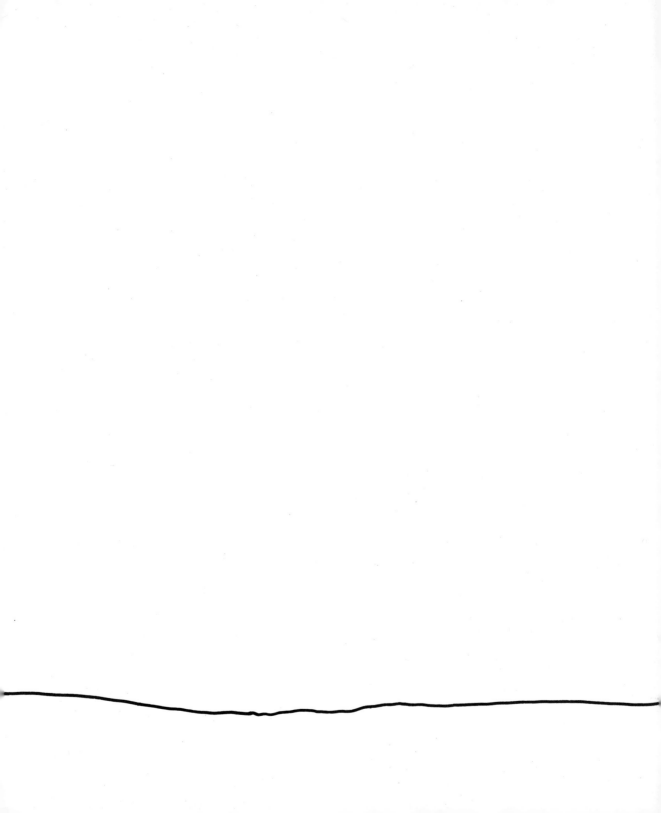

Some fit...

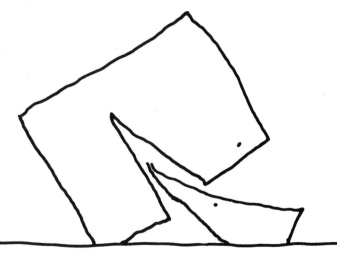

but could not roll.

Others could roll
but did not fit.

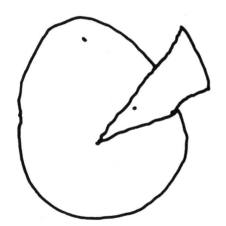

One didn't know a thing about fitting.

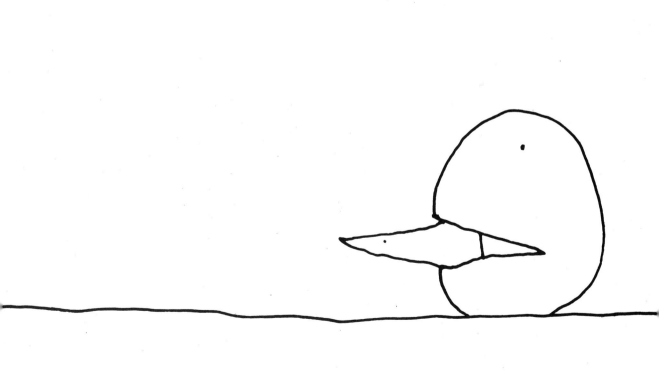

And another
didn't know a thing
about anything.

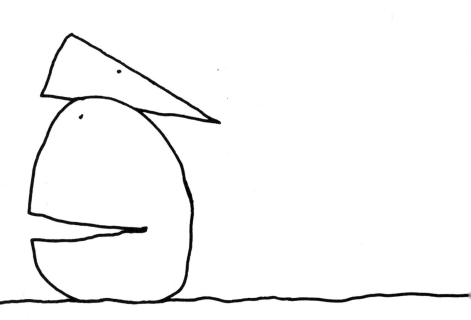

One was too delicate.

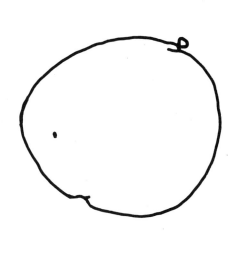

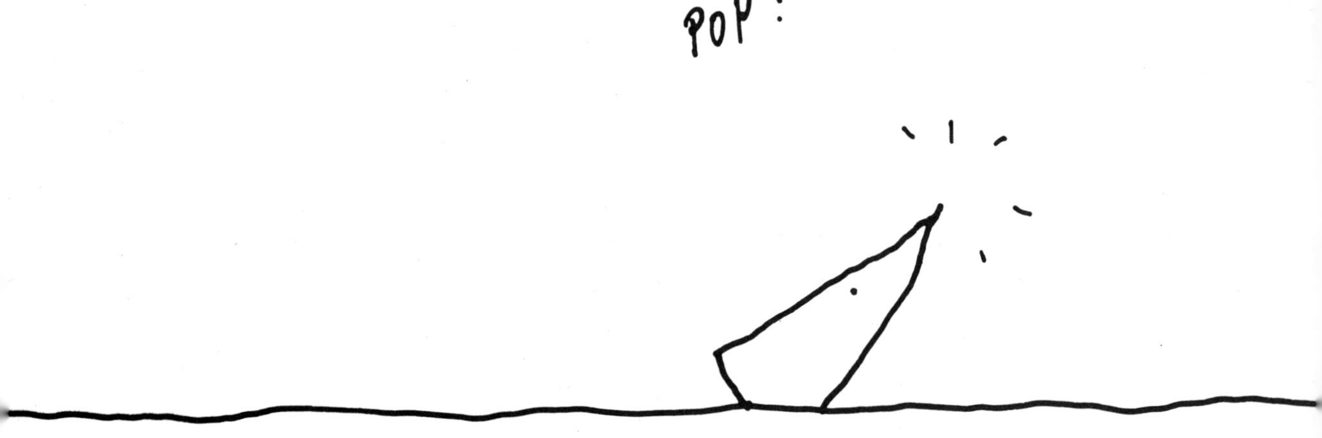
POP!

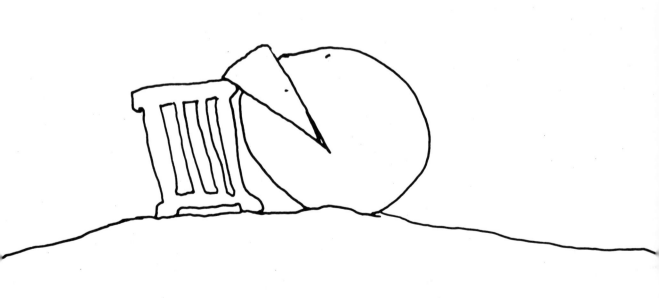

One put it on a pedestal...

and left it there.

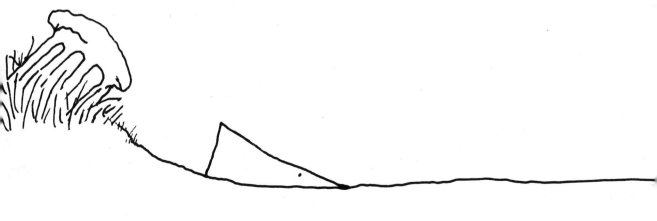

It learned to hide from the hungry ones.

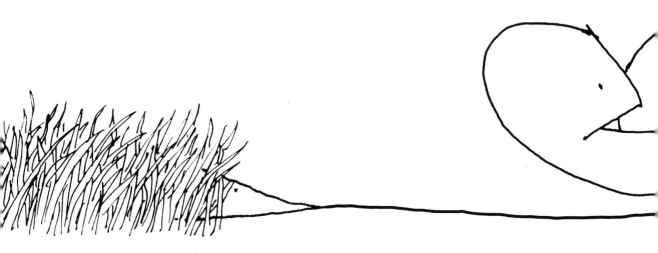

Some had too many pieces, period.

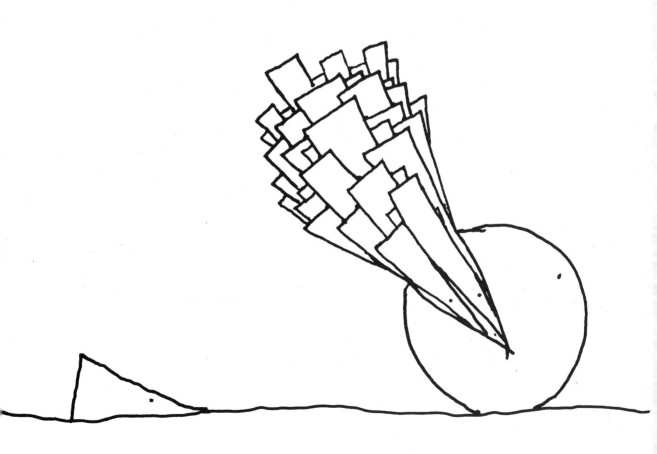

Some had too many pieces missing.

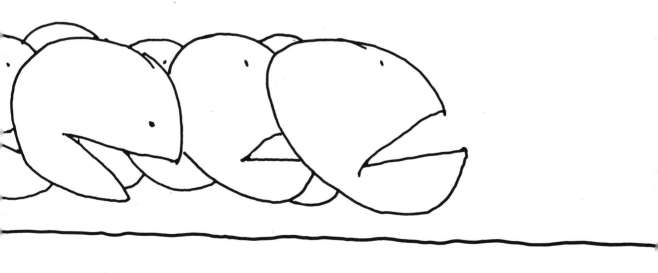

More came.

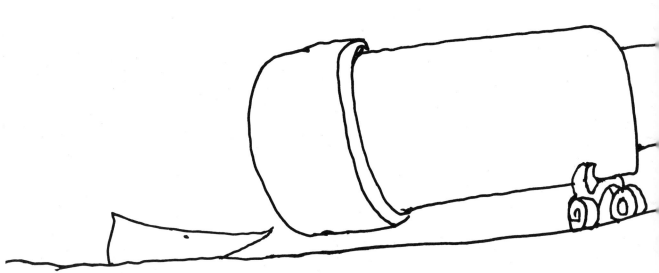

Some looked too closely.

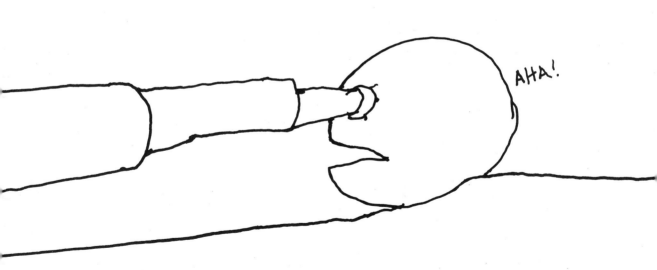

Others rolled right by without noticing.

HI..?

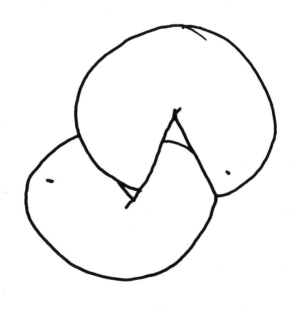

It tried to make itself
more attractive....

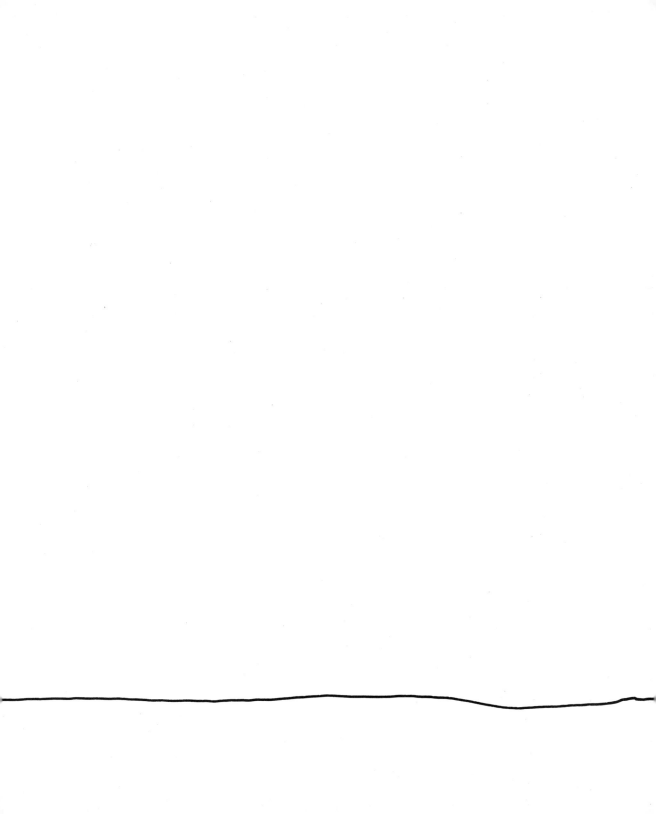

It didn't help.

It tried being flashy

the missing piece began to grow!

And grow!

"I didn't know
  you were going
  to grow."

"I didn't know it either,"
said the missing piece.

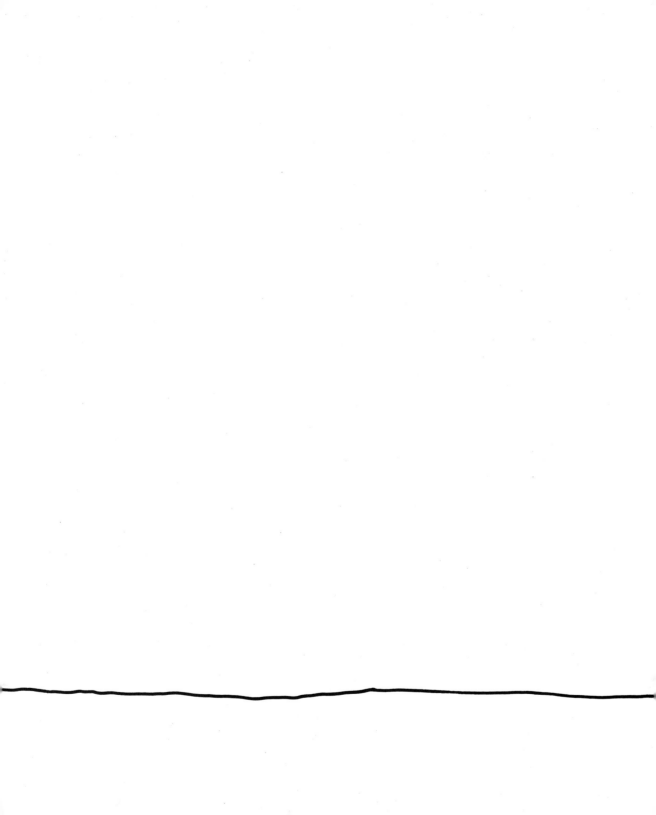

BYE...

"I'm lookin' for
my missin' piece,
one that won't
increase...."

SIGH....

And then one day,

one came along who looked different.

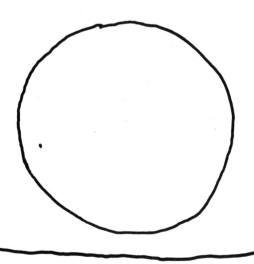

"What do you want of me?"
asked the missing piece.

"Nothing."

"What do you need from me?"

"Nothing."

"Who are you?" asked the missing piece.

"I am the Big O,"
said the Big O.

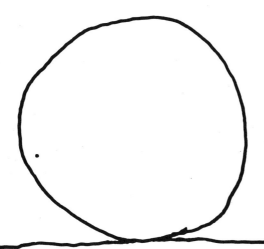

"I think you are the one
  I have been waiting for,"
  said the missing piece.
"Maybe I am your missing piece."

"But I am not missing a piece,"
  said the Big O.
"There is no place you would fit."

"That is too bad," said the missing piece.
"I was hoping that perhaps
  I could roll with you...."

"You cannot roll with me,"
  said the Big O,
"but perhaps you can roll by yourself."

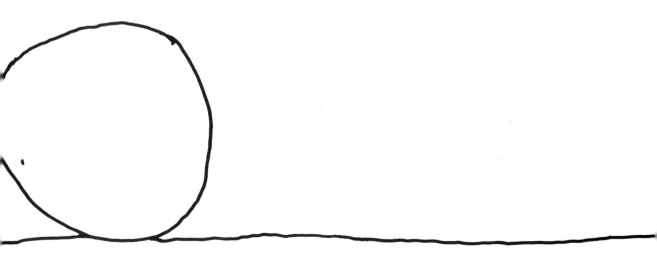

"By myself?
    A missing piece cannot
    roll by itself."

"But I have sharp corners,"
said the missing piece.
"I am not shaped for rolling."

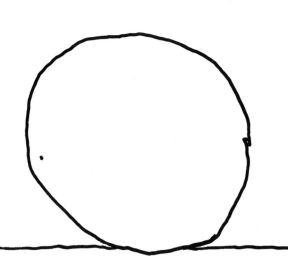

"Have you ever tried?"
asked the Big O.

"Corners wear off,"
  said the Big O,
"and shapes change.
  Anyhow, I must say good-bye.
  Perhaps we will meet again...."

And away it rolled.

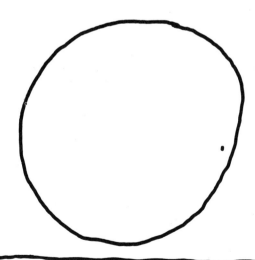

The missing piece
was alone again.

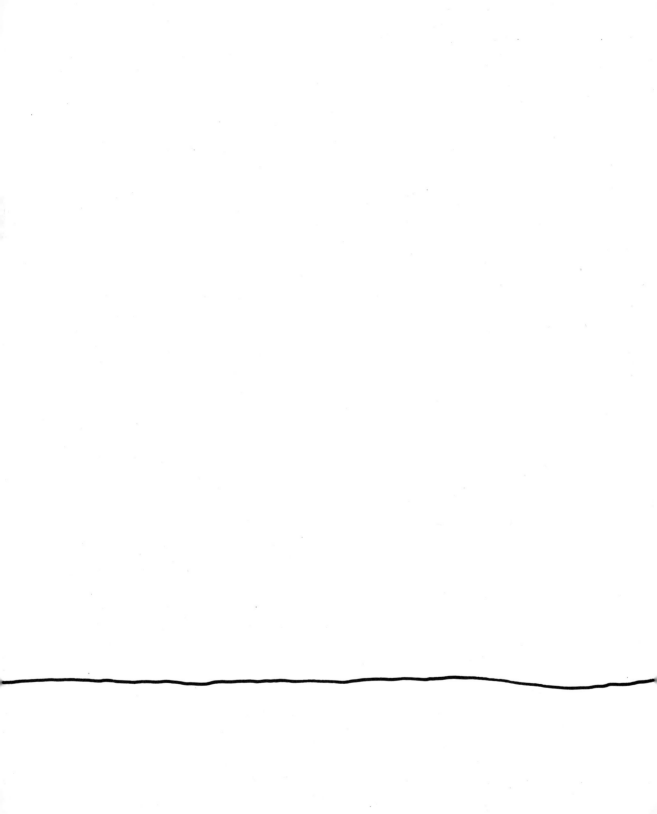

For a long time
it just sat there.

Then...
slowly...
it lifted itself up on one end...

…and flopped over.

PLOP!

Then lift…pull…flop…

it began to move forward....

And soon its edges began to wear off....

liftpullflopliftpullflop...

and its shape began to change...

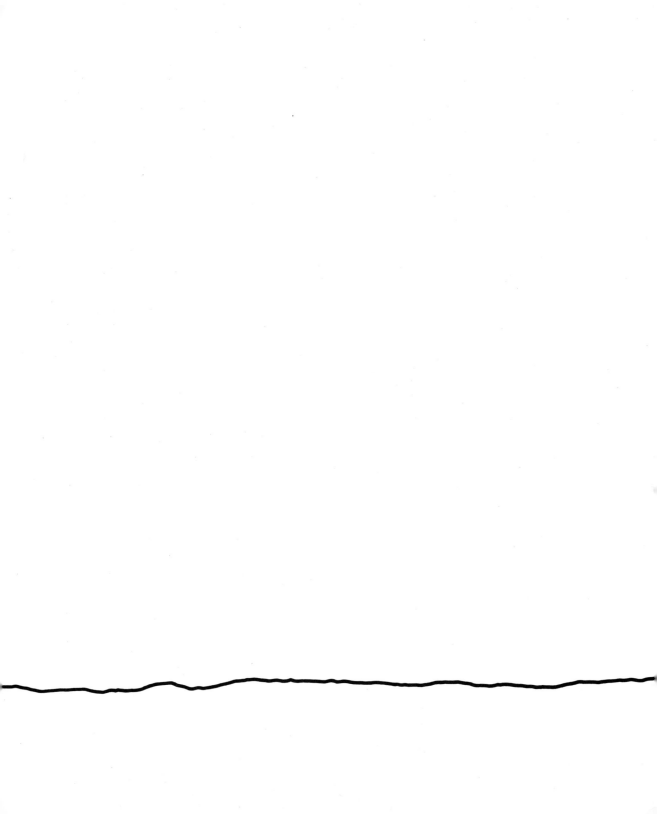

and then it was bumping instead of flopping...

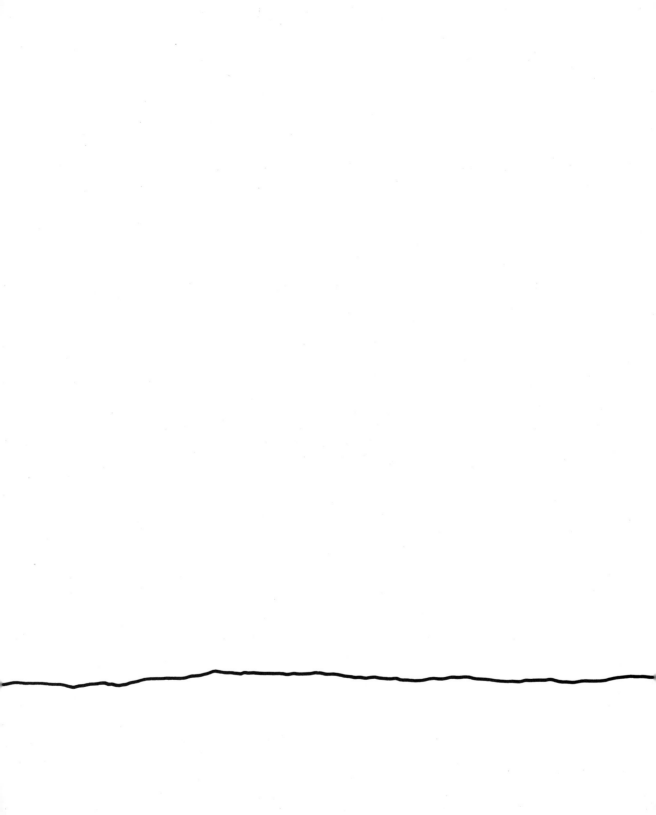

and then it was bouncing instead of bumping...

and then it was rolling instead of bouncing....

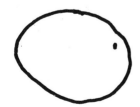

And it didn't know where
and it didn't care.

It was rolling!

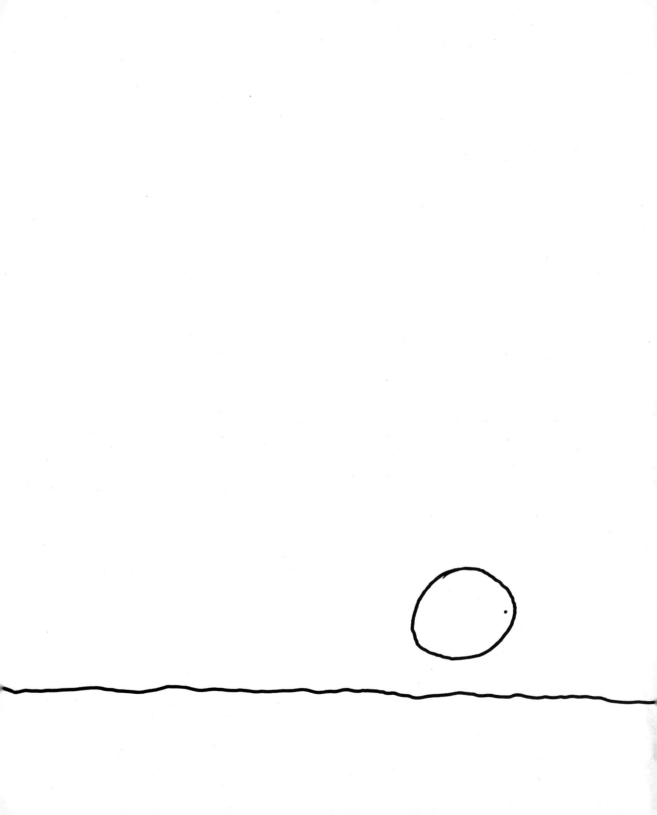

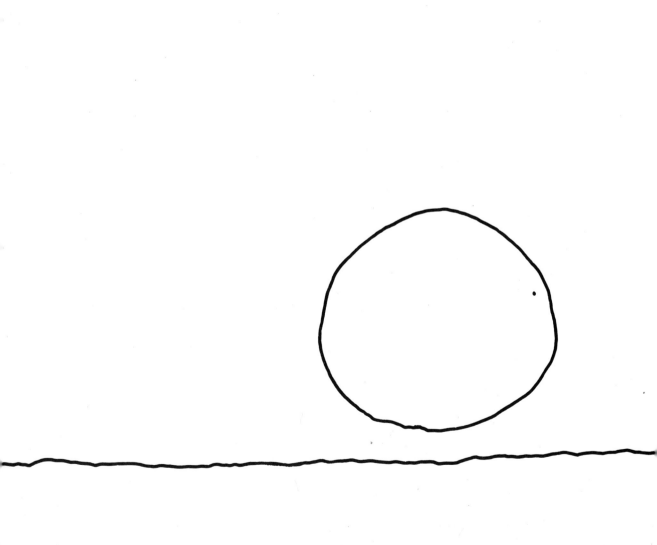

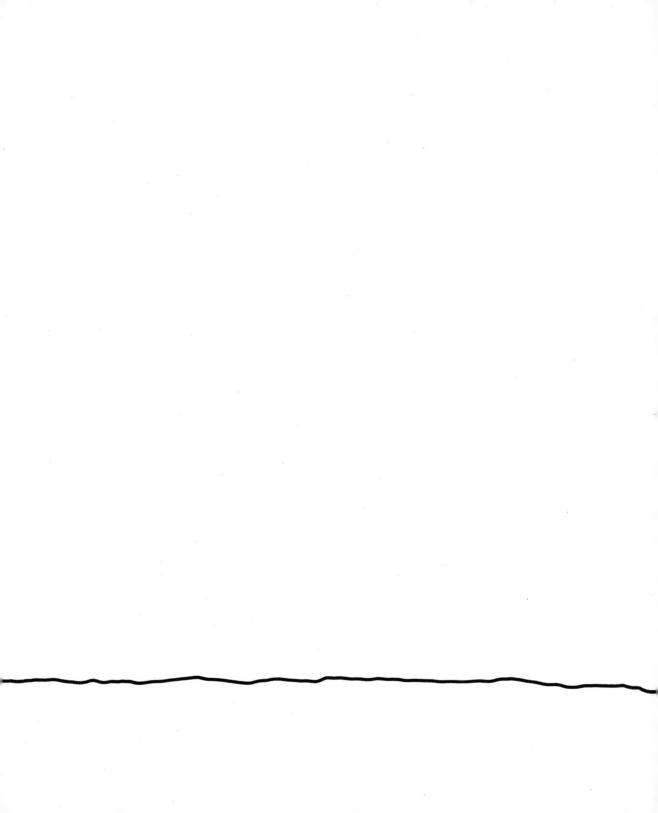

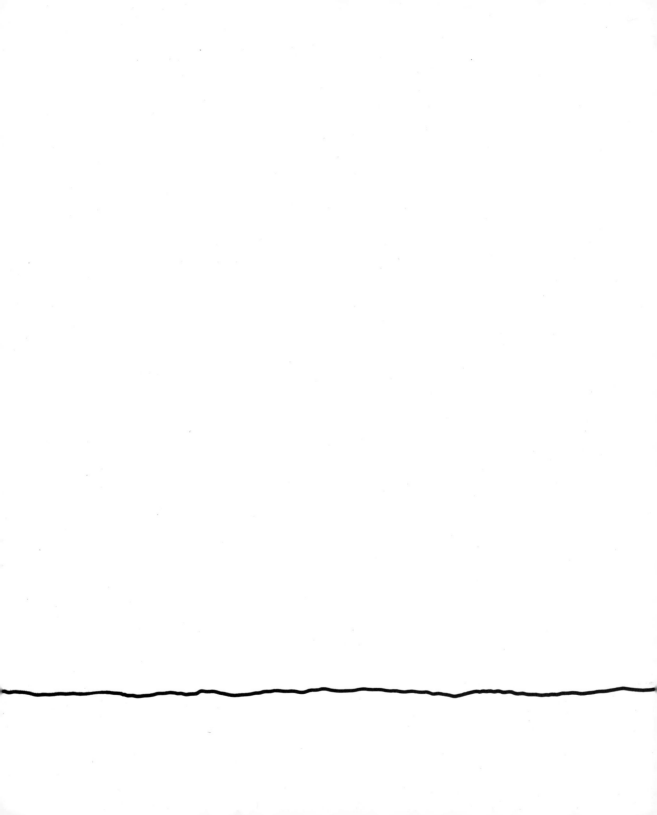

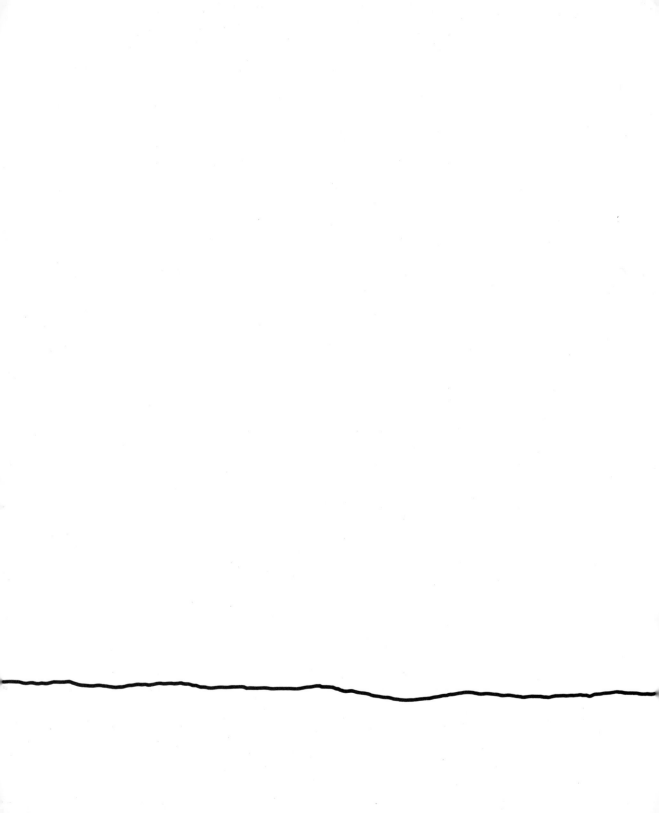